HOUSE
on the
ROOF

The HOUSE on the ROOF

A SUKKOT STORY

By
David A. Adler

Pictures by
Marilyn Hirsh

KAR-BEN COPIES, INC.   ROCKVILLE, MD

TO OUR VERY SPECIAL MUTTI

Library of Congress Cataloging in Publication Data

Adler, David A.
  The house on the roof.

  Reprint. Originally published: New York: Bonim
Books, cl976.
  Summary: Despite the protests of his landlady, an old
man builds a Sukkah for himself and his grandchildren on
the roof of an apartment building.
  1. Children's stories, American. [1. Sukkoth—Fiction.
2. Jews—United States—Fiction] I. Hirsh, Marilyn, ill.
II. Title.
PZ7.A2615Ho 1984   [E]   84-12555

ISBN 0-930494-35-0 (pbk.)

One day,
the old man from apartment 3D
dragged a heavy
wood crate
up the front steps
of his building.

"Don't scratch the paint
with that junk,"
the owner of the building yelled.
"I don't have the halls painted
so you can scratch the paint right off."

The next day,
the old man collected
acorns and autumn leaves.

When he brought them into the building,
the owner yelled from her window,
"Don't drop anything.
If someone falls and gets hurt
I'll be the one to pay."

He collected old magazines
and the owner yelled,
"Junk
and more junk.
Most people throw it out.
You collect it."

The old man collected more crates . . .

old clothes . . .
empty bottles . . .
and broken branches.

He brought everything
into the building.
Each time he walked
up the front steps
the owner yelled.

For more than a week,
inside his small apartment,
the old man hammered
and sewed and polished.

Then,
one evening,
just before sunset,
the old man left the building.
He was wearing his suit and derby hat.
The owner sat by her window and watched.

About an hour later, he returned.
He was talking and laughing.
His grandchildren were with him.
They were talking and laughing, too.

They followed the old man
up the front steps
and into the building.

The owner followed them.

They walked up three flights of stairs,
past the old man's apartment,
and onto the roof.

In the corner,
there was a small hut.
The walls were made of wood crates.
The roof was made of broken branches.

Inside was a small table
covered with a patchwork cloth.
The cloth was made of torn clothes.
Candles burned in candlesticks.
The candlesticks were made of old bottles.
Chains of acorns and autumn leaves
hung from the roof.
On the walls were pictures
cut from old magazines.
On the table there was wine,
soda, cake, and cookies.

"Wow!"
"Beautiful,"
the children said.
"This is the most beautiful Sukkah."

The old man smiled.

The old man drank wine.
The children drank soda
and a little wine.
They all ate cake and cookies.

"OFF!"
the owner yelled.
"OFF MY ROOF!
I rent you an apartment,
not a roof.
And take that junk with you."

She started swinging her broom
and chasing them.
"Take that junk down," she yelled.
"Get off my roof."

The old man and his grandchildren
ran from the roof.
But the old man did not
take his Sukkah down.

A few days later,
the owner of the building
brought the old man to court.

"It's my building
and my roof,"
she told the judge.

"Well,"
the judge asked the old man,
"what do you have to say?"

"Your Honor," the old man answered,
"thousands of years ago, my people were slaves in Egypt.
When they escaped to the desert,
they had no time to build homes.
As they traveled, they built temporary huts.
Each autumn, we celebrate the holiday of Sukkot
by building and living in huts just like theirs.
That's what I did.
Now in only four days
the holiday will be over.
I would like so much to keep my Sukkah
for just that long.

The judge thought and thought.

Then he turned to the owner.
"You're right,"
he said to her.
"It is your building.
No one should be allowed to build on your roof
without your permission."

Then the judge said
to the old man,
"I'll give you just ten days
to take your Sukkah down."
The judge smiled.

"Ten days,"
the old man thought.
Then he smiled, too.